Tales of the Sisters Kane

-Book I-

To Jauna,
Hope you enjoy the Tales!
Christy Kane
2.25.07

by: Christy Kane

Baby Tattoo Books®

Copyright © 2006 Christy Kane

"Baby Tattoo," "Baby Tattoo Books" and logo are trademarks of Baby Tattoo Books®.

ISBN-13 978-0-9778949-4-9

ISBN-10 0-9778949-4-0

Library of Congress Control Number: 2006905898

First Edition

10 9 8 7 6 5 4 3 2 1

Published by Baby Tattoo Books®
Los Angeles, California
www.babytattoo.com
Manufactured in China

Book design by Christy Kane and Miwa Nishio
Text edited by Rani Self & Judie Brown
Photo of Christy by Sharon Preen
Thank you to my family and friends for their constant support.
Thank you also to the Self family.
Lastly, thank you to my cousin Shirley Akers
for helping me find the city we love.

Contents

To Mom and Dad with love.

INTRODUCTION

The Sisters Kane, after many years, have decided to share their tales, some of which are unsettling to a few readers. If you are one of those readers -- that is fine! Pass this book on to the black sheep of your family as he or she is bound to relate.

These stories are meant to entertain and to teach valuable life lessons. They are also true stories. These dolls do exist and they are all sisters. . . and I am their mother.

So find a cozy seat, have a cup of tea and read on. The dolls thank you endlessly for your utmost attention.

Christy Kane

❀ LILY ❀

Meet lovely Lily and listen well,
heed the words which I now tell.

A lesson could make you think twice
about ignoring sound advice.

Lily chose to ignore her mother
one time, two times, and another.

She'd been told to "Stay away.
Sewing machines are not for play,

no, not for girls your age and size."
"Yes, dear Mother" Lily replied.

Yet did she listen...you ask me?
No, not at all as you will see.

Her mother, one sunny afternoon,
went picking flowers fresh in bloom,

out in the garden, which was not near
any windows for her to hear

her sewing machine clinking about,
or Lily if she were to shout.

All alone with her mother outside,
and ignoring her voice inside,

Lily decided to mend a dress
so her doll Agatha could look her best.

She found some thread and some lace
and carefully put it all in place.

She stacked some books on the chair
and hopped up top without a care.

She began at the count of three
and tragedy struck instantly.

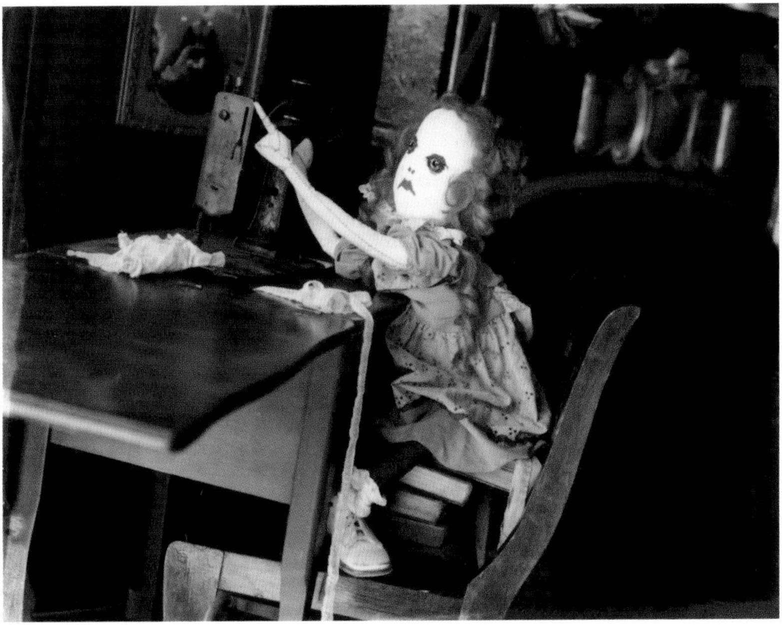

Lily decided to mend a dress

In not paying attention to detail at all,
and since her hands were very small,

the utter force of the machine, you see,
was just too much for poor Lily.

The thread wound round her finger tight
for she had not laid the fabric right.

The pressure and pain quickly grew.
She fretted "Oh what shall I do?"

She quickly drew her hand away
and her arm did fall, but to her dismay,
wound in the thread her finger lay.

"Sewing machines are not for play."

❀ She fretted "Oh what shall I do?" ❀

In disbelief she wrapped her hand

in fabric which she had planned

to use for Agatha's little dress.

Instead she was in quite a mess.

She wandered to the window rail

and sat there pouting, growing pale.

❋ Instead she was in quite a mess ❋

Just then Mother opened the door

and dropped her flowers on the floor.

She cried, "Sweet Lily not again!

Nine times, now let's not make it ten!"

For this had happened eight times before.

Gentle Lily, who all did adore,

had lost a finger on this day

using a sewing machine for play.

And when asked why she did it at all

she'd say in a voice both sweet and small,

"I'm aware that I do not sew well

but my desire begins to swell.

I can not control the urge to sew

and though my mother tells me no,

I find a way and as you see

I learn my lessons tragically."

So heed the warning, reader dear,

if told of something "Do not go near."

Perhaps those words are sound advice

and will aid you in thinking twice.

Attention naysayers:

(A quick reality check for those who
judge the mother in question)

Who would leave a child alone
with danger lurking in the home?

"No, not I" cried the people loud
with boisterous voices bold and proud.

But people you must face the facts
that life is full of little acts.

"Accidents" is what they are called
and everybody big and small

cannot deny that they are real.
When they occur we each must deal.

They happen to everyone without fail.
No real protection is for sale.

For accident does just imply
no one's to blame, not you or I.

So if you say Lily's mother is to blame,
think of when you've heard the same

about somebody, or even yourself
when what took place no one could help.

Because in life you rise and you fall
whether you're a person or a doll.

❈ POLLY ❈

At the ripe age of fifteen Polly was given a shiny new pair of roller-skates. They were bright white with gorgeous blue wheels. She immediately put them on her feet and in no time went tearing down the road. It was as if she'd been made to roller-skate. Turns were no problem, and she kept her speed under control. Never before could she remember having such a nice time; no, nothing she had ever done measured up to this.

"I will skate forever, until the earth ceases to spin. I will skate forever!" It was precisely at this moment that she ran right into a rosebush. You see she was a bit of a day-dreamer, and it did cost her on occasion.

"Ouch" she cried out. Rosebushes are just full of thorns, and they were not retractable, you see, so Polly got numerous scrapes. "Well, no bother," she said with the utmost confidence. "I will keep on skating, scrapes or no scrapes" and indeed, she did.

Soon night fell, and she was so excited to be skating in the moonlight! For about half a second, Polly thought of skating back home, but what a mundane choice when the whole world was out there waiting. "Why go home, when instead I can skate the sun up and down every day. I won't go back. I will skate across the world and back. I will greet the seasons with my wheels, forever and ever!"

It was not long before day was breaking. Polly realized she had entered a new town. She was impressed with all the trees. She thought to herself how easy it had been to skate into a new town, and it had only taken her one day.

Day after day Polly skated, never thinking of anything but how wondrous it was to be living daily atop eight beautiful blue wheels. However, she sometimes found herself encountering obstacles, some more trying than others. Her thought process was that of a daydreamer. And although she could have benefited from a spoonful or two of common sense, she managed just the same.

On one occasion she found herself in the forest. It was the height of autumn and the forest was full of color. She marveled at the falling leaves and pressed on through the thick grove. Little did she know she would soon be falling like the leaves. A terrible wind storm seemed to come out of nowhere. She found herself fighting the wind, which proved for Polly to be a losing battle. For awhile she did pretty well skating from tree to tree, holding onto them as tightly as she could. But between two pines and an oak Polly was blown right to the ground!

✻ A terrible windstorm seemed to come out of nowhere ✻

❧ She found herself fighting the wind ❧

"Ouch!" This time she landed on her chin. "Oh well, at least my skates are okay" she thought to herself. She decided to wait out the wind storm, so she laid on the ground watching the leaves as they were blown in all sorts of directions. Soon enough the forest was still and Polly made her way out, safe and sound.

Onward she went… and she went far.

A new town everyday, and before she knew it she found herself in a beautiful meadow full of blooming poppies. They were bright orange and smelled so sweet that she decided to spend the whole day there. She skated through mazes of poppies, all the while singing and laughing in her carefree state. You can imagine her surprise when her wheel became caught in a snake hole. This one really hurt. . . "What a terrible accident," she thought. Not only was she in pain, but she was utterly sad to find she had crushed a fair amount of poppies. "Well, what to do? I suppose I could just rest for awhile." And that she did.

She napped long enough that the sun had the opportunity to rise and set four times. "That's plenty of rest, now I had better be going. Goodbye dear poppies. I feel I will

❀ What a terrible accident ❀

see you soon enough!" And the poppies bid her farewell, as only flowers can do. Quietly and beautifully, saying nothing and everything, only to be off in their own world again soaking up the sun in an instant.

Polly skated for two days and could not believe how chilly it was getting. She figured it would pass, but she was wrong. Out of nowhere the air filled with perfect little snow flakes. She could not believe it was possible that snow could be a mere two day skate away from sunny fields and poppies! She wondered if the poppies would like the snow, and she imagined that if she knew anything about knitting she would surely turn back and knit every flower a little bonnet to keep them all warm.

She then thought of the matter at hand. Skating in the snow. Initially, she thought the snow would be easy to skate on top of, and it was for awhile, but as night fell, the snow flakes multiplied by the thousands. All of a sudden she was stuck in a blizzard, and her wheels were quick to freeze.

Polly was not discouraged. In her spirited but chilly mind she knew the snow would melt, so she decided to just enjoy it.

❀ She was stuck in a blizzard ❀

❀ and her wheels were quick to freeze ❀

❀ She knew the snow would melt ❀

✤ Then she took a well deserved nap ✤

She fell forward and made some snow angels for fun. She built a little snowman and told it of her adventures to date. Then she took a well deserved nap.

Upon waking, she saw the beaming sun was fast at work melting the snow, and she reached down and gave her wheels a spin. That was that, it was time to move on.

She found a road and without delay, she was skating at top speed. She must have skated a very long time, because she realized she was seeing her fifth full moon.

The air that had once been chilly was now replaced with hot dry air. It was so hot in fact that Polly was skating at her slowest pace yet. She looked around and saw nothing for miles. Nothing but sand and peculiar trees that seemed to be confused as to whether or not they were trees or cacti. She thought they were quite the phenomenon and imagined they must have been around for millions of years. She asked one if it had ever seen roller-skates before and she took its silent response for a "no." She felt obligated to skate through the entire desert and introduce all of the cacti-trees to roller-skates. So she did.

❀ She looked around and saw nothing for miles ❀

This venture took her a good many days, and when she felt she was done, she rested under the biggest cacti-tree she could find. After some contemplation, Polly decided to take a good long look at her wheels. They had been through such a variety of elements and she hoped they were not suffering any. Each wheel looked as strong and blue as it had on her fifteenth birthday. She was delighted. "I will truly be able to skate forever," she thought to herself.

And she is well on her way to accomplishing that. In fact, I can report that she is still skating as we speak. She skates past my window about the same time every year. It is always nearing Easter so the Easter Bunny leaves her basket with me. Polly always stops in for tea, eats a chocolate bunny, and tells me her newest adventures.

Her biggest surprise that she shared with me this year is that she met her first fairy. She said the fairy was a sweet little lass who directed Polly to a grove full of strawberries. Polly had herself a feast of fruit.

❧ This year . . . she met her first fairy ❧

I told her the same thing I tell her every year; she should write her own book telling of the marvels she has seen. But she says it would really be too bothersome because she would have to stop skating for too long in order to write it all down.

If you want to know more about her adventures I suggest looking out your window. You may be lucky enough to spot her. If you are curious about whether she has seen this or that, I think it is safe to say she probably has. She is always happy to share her tales, so just call out her name and ask away. And in case you are also wondering just how long she has been roller-skating, I can report that as of last Easter, Miss Polly was 112 years old. Amazingly enough, she looks not a day over 15, and shows no sign of slowing down. In fact, I can say with confidence that she could easily out skate any of us if ever given the chance.

❃ . . .the marvels she has seen ❃

❈ CALLALILLY ❈

Callalilly longed to play
on the piano night and day,

complex pieces, sonnets too.
She hoped one day to play them through.

But to truly hone your skill
one must have tremendous will.

One must practice every day
which sometimes means foregoing play.

Practice means less time for tea
which sat not well with Callalilly.

She wanted the skill to be innate.
She wanted to be instantly great,

to play on pianos great and small
with seemingly no effort at all.

Yet when she sat down to play
it all came out the wrong way.

❧ To play on pianos great and small
with seemingly no effort at all ❧

If the song was written in the key of "C"
it read "B-flat" to Callalilly.

Oh the sound was grim at best
which put her patience to the test!

She would try again, and get it wrong.
She simply could not play a song.

It seemed to her, her little hands
could not meet with her demands.

"One more wrong note" she said aloud
"and I will smash this cover down!"

One more wrong note came right away,
so Callalilly, without delay

smashed down the cover, but not in time
to free her hand from this temper crime.

❀ One more wrong note came right away ❀

49

She realized on that fateful day
she should have behaved a different way.

She should have been patient with herself.
She should have asked someone for help.

But alas, it was now too late.
She had sadly sealed her fate.

Her left hand paid the price
for not playing the sonnet right.

So that, dear reader of this book,
is why Callalilly has a hook

in the place of her left hand
that failed to meet her mind's demand.

❊ Her left hand paid the price ❊

You might think that it left her sad,
or such a state would leave her mad.

But neither emotion does she feel
despite the fact that is quite real,

that she now has but one hand
because her temper was so grand.

Her acceptance now begins to grow.
Her two best friends have told me so.

Clarabelle and Annabelle
assure me that she is doing well.

❃ Clarabelle and Annabelle ❃

In fact, to their utter surprise
her desire to play is on the rise.

She decided to give it another try,
this time staying calm inside.

With practice she found to her delight
that she CAN play the sonnets right.

The left hand notes she just ignores
and plays the parts that she adores.

She now writes songs for her friends,
which delights them to no end.

So the lesson, I'm sure you see,
learned by little Callalilly,

is that a temper if not tamed
can leave a little rag doll maimed.

And this goes the same for people too.
So one last thought before I'm through,

"Please dear reader, whatever you do,
don't let your temper get the best of you."

✻ She's writing songs for her friends ✻

AND NOW. . .
INTRODUCING THE THE TRIPLETS
AND THEIR BABY SISTER
WISTERIA

�֍ HYACINTH �֍

59

❦ AZAELEAH ❦

❦ VIOLAH ❧

❧ WISTERIA ❧

Triplets are not too common, it seems, especially triplets so absolutely dissimilar. Such is the case with the Kane girls from a little town deep in the South called Alaflora. Now they are not different across the board; they do have some things in common including their love of autumn, butterflies and strawberry jam. But when you look at them it is fairly obvious which one is the "trouble-maker". And this, of course, is Violah. The three girls came into the world like the rest of us; with their personalities already intact.

Hyacinth, the reflective, deep thinker was scheduled to be born first. Violah, who had decided she wished she had been an only child, was to be born second. And Azaeleah, who would not blame a bee for stinging her, was to be third in line. Azaeleah was the gentlest of souls with an inability to see fault, which as you will later read, eventually cost her greatly. Their birthday transpired as follows.

It was four in the morning. The moon and the sun were at odds about who should take over, and the air had a peculiar chill. Hyacinth, positioned to be first, prepared herself for birth. At the very instant she was to be born, she felt an unnatural tug on her leg. Not knowing what to do, she pulled with all her might to free her leg from whatever it may have been stuck on. It was not until she felt an excruciating pain that the grim reality of what was going on revealed itself to Hyacinth. She spotted her sister Violah, who had an unnatural hold on Hyacinth's leg. Her face was rigid as she continued pulling on Hyacinth's leg, ultimately pulling it off entirely.

As Hyacinth bellowed in agony Violah forged ahead and was the first born. You can imagine the shock when Hyacinth was next, and her leg was completely detached.

In those days, stitching of that magnitude was set aside for seamstresses, so Hyacinth was given a peg.

Azaeleah was last, and you are probably wondering what this sweet little soul thought of what had just taken place. To tell you the truth, she had slept through it. It was Hyacinth's cry that woke her up. Azaeleah refused to believe Violah would have done such a thing. She said Hyacinth must have caught her leg on something, or that perhaps her leg was never really attached all that well in the first place.

Violah reveled in glory realizing she had gotten away with such a dastardly act. She even decided to nick name herself : The Silent Terror.

As the triplets went through their early years, Hyacinth

✺ In those days, stitching of that magnitude was set aside
for seamstresses, so Hyacinth was given a peg ✺

was all but too aware that Violah could not be trusted and did her best to protect little Azaeleah. She was frequently afraid of her sister Violah, for obvious reasons. As frustrated as she would get, she still knew better than to cross her.

At the top of the list of Hyacinth's duties was keeping a close eye on their younger sister Wisteria. She was a tiny little lass with an ailment that inhibited her ability to grow. She was destined to be miniature so Hyacinth took care to keep her delicate little sister out of Violah's reach. Taking this into account, Violah waited for Wisteria to have a bad morning. She knew if little Wisteria were to fall into a crying fit, Hyacinth would be pre-occupied with Wisteria and Violah could coax Azaeleah out into the woods. This fateful day came to pass in December of 1743.

Wisteria had been taunted by Violah as her sisters slept and tore into a great fit of sobbing. Hyacinth awoke and ran to her aid. She tried to calm her with little success. This was why she could not join Violah and Azaeleah on their morning walk, even though she feared something dreadful could possibly happen.

❁ She watched the wide-eyed Azaeleah ❁

71

Wisteria sobbed on and Hyacinth tried her best to soothe the little one, masking her own desire to sob while she watched the wide-eyed Azaeleah hold onto Violah's arm as they went into the woods.

As soon as Azaleah and Violah were out of sight, Wisteria calmed down. Sadly, she could not speak to tell Hyacinth of Violah's taunting, but Hyacinth had a good idea Violah was behind Wisterias tears. She held her tiny sister and decided she had better go after the other two, mainly to protect Azaeleah or "Zaeley" as Hyacinth called her. She got out Wisteria's stroller and went up into the attic to fetch an old bird cage she had spotted weeks before. She put a warm blanket inside and then fit her tiny sister through the cage door. Her final step was putting a lock on the door. She locked Wisteria safely inside put the key on a ribbon and wore it around her neck. The cage fit perfectly into Wisteria's carriage, and Hyacinth felt sure she would be safe from Violah.

"You will be safe in there little Wisteria, and there is no way Violah will get this key!" she said, assuring herself mainly. She hurried down the grassy hill and headed toward the path in the woods where her sisters had ventured. Frantically, and unsuccessfully, she searched the woods.

❄ Hyacinth had a good idea Violah was behind the chaos ❄

73

Meanwhile, in a different part of the forest, Violah pulled Azaleah by the arm. "This way Zaeley, I've got something for you." They traipsed through the thick grass and over thorny twigs to a little opening in the forest where there was a beautiful flower garden. "Oh Violah, it's so lovely!" Zaeley cried. She dove head-first into a flower bed in search of ladybugs, and then said, "I do hope we see some butterflies!"

Violah, on top of many other things, was a very jealous creature. She could not stand the attention Hyacinth got for her lovely locks and delicate manner. Even worse, she loathed Azaleah's innocence. It drove her mad! She knew nothing she could say or do would make Azaleah turn on her. Besides Azaeleah's inno-cence, Violah felt she was too flawless for her own good. Hyacinth had lost her leg which made Violah feel a bit superior to her, but Zaeley, by Violah's standards, was just TOO perfect.

Violah gazed off momentarily, re-evaluating her plan. She looked around, and saw all the thorny branches, and knew her plan was bound to work. She pasted on a phony look of distress and called out in her best melo-dramatic tone, "Azaeleah come quickly, I seem to have caught my arm on this branch!"

Azaeleah shot up and ran to her aid. "Let me see if I can help" she said in her gentle voice. She could not see where her sisters' arm was caught, so she went in for a closer look. Just then Violah pulled her hand, releasing a gnarly branch that flew into Azaleah's face with such great force it snatched her left eye out of its socket.

Her cry was so loud Hyacinth heard her clear across the woods. In no time she had made her way to the "accident."

"My poor sister," Violah cried. "What a terrible thing has happened! You poor, poor thing."

Naive girl that Azaeleah was, she leaned on her sister for support and said, "At least your arm is alright." This comment made Violah flinch with remorse for half a mili-second.

"I knew it!" Hyacinth said, glaring at Violah.

"Knew what!" Violah replied in her normal venomous tone.

"Nothing. . .I just felt that you two might be in trouble. Call it an instinct," Hyacinth said.

Violah, who longed to laugh out loud, for she was a sick twisted girl, put on a coy face. "Why don't I take Wisteria, and you can help Azaeleah" she offered.

Hyacinth felt the key about her neck and said "Fine."

Violah raced ahead with the little one. Her dismay was immeasurable as she saw the lock on the cage. She anxiously considered a variety of ways to get to Wisteria, but figured she was going to have to bide her time. She slowed her pace and strolled toward home, thinking how grand it was that of the three sisters she was now the most "flawless."

Hyacinth was quite unaffected by that which others might perceive as gory. She calmly looked all around for her sister's eye, and ended up finding it on a branch full of thorns. "Zaeley, I am afraid your poor eye is a bit like my leg. It doesn't look like it can be saved."

Azaeleah sighed, "That's fine. I am sure you can mend me somehow and it will be okay. You are the best seamstress I know!" The two slowly walked home and upon

76

❀ Azaeleah was quite pleased ❀

77

their arrival Hyacinth went right to her sewing box. She made a fine patch and sewed it over the former dwelling place of Azaeleah's left eye. She fetched a mirror and Azaeleah was quite pleased.

For several months that followed, Violah was unbearably nice. Azaeleah of course failed to notice, but Hyacinth became exceedingly concerned. She now kept Wisteria in the bird cage at all times!

❋ She now kept Wisteria in the bird cage at all times ❋

Hyacinth's knack for being responsible weighed heavily on her at times, for she was the only sister who remained calm in the shadows of danger. Every summer Hyacinth prepared for the storms. They would come out of nowhere and on occasion take a roof-top or a tree away in their windy clutches. Such a storm was on the way on the night of August 3rd, 1745. The windows were rattling and the tree branches were knocking against the house. Even Violah was panicking, or so she claimed. Hyacinth had to go board up the windows, and bring in all the flower pots. Wisteria was wailing more than usual and Hyacinth made a fateful decision. She handed Azaeleah the key to Wisteria's cage and told her to go and get her little sister out and rock her for awhile.

Hyacinth gave strict orders for Azaeleah to carefully hide the key in her old shoe box and make sure Violah did not see. Although Azaeleah was naive, she could see the serious look in Hyacinth's eyes and for the first time in her dolly life, she took on a protective feeling toward Wisteria. She did as Hyacinth said, and it calmed Wisteria down. She put her back in the cage and put the lock back on the door. She looked around and it seemed as though the coast was clear. But Azaeleah, as you have just read, had what one might refer to as a blind spot. So as sure as she was that Violah was nowhere near, she was terribly mistaken.

As she put the key into Hyacinth's old shoe box, she felt quite sure that she had been very responsible. Unfortunately, Violah was right behind her, spying through a hole in the curtains. What happened next is a mystery. . .

Azaelah greeted Hyacinth and told her she had done exactly what she had been asked to do. The two then went about locking all the windows, as the storm approached. Meanwhile Violah was plotting away upstairs. She took the key and paused to bask in her success. She had been patient as she knew eventually the other two would slip up. She knew Hyacinth could not wear that key forever, and she had been waiting for a long time, writing in her journal each time she devised a different plan for getting hold of Wisteria.

❦ Violah spies ❦

Now she had her chance. It was not long before the storm came and the sisters gathered together to wait it out. Hyacinth asked Azaeleah to go and get Wisteria, and moments later she heard a shriek of horror. She and Violah darted into the room to see what was wrong and there was the bird cage. The door was wide open and their little sister was nowhere to be seen.

Hyacinth glared at Violah who coyly said, "Wherever could little Wisteria be?"

The sisters frantically searched, but to no avail. Violah eventually fell asleep and Hyacinth decided to investigate further.

She found Violah's journal, and read how she had been plotting to capture Wisteria and hide her away somewhere where no one could ever find her. Her descriptions were vague but creepy. She used a ridiculous amount of adjectives to glamorize her proposed wicked behavior.

Azaeleah wandered in and found Hyacinth nearing tears. They went in and looked for Hyacinth's key but it was gone. Azaeleah fell to the floor. She felt certain it was her fault. Hyacinth tried to console her, and

assured Zaeley that they would find Wisteria. She herself could not imagine where to begin the search.
As horrible as Violah was, she was pretty sure she would not do anything too terrible to Wisteria. But as she gazed at her now one eyed sister, she was far from convinced.

The next day was somber. The two sisters questioned Violah with no success. She swore up and down that she had not seen or heard a thing. And she was happy to point out that Azaeleah had been the last to hold the little dear.

"Perhaps Azaeleah and Wisteria are playing some twisted joke?" Violah queried.

Azaeleah was horrified at this suggestion and burst into tears.

Hyacinth tried to calm her as the three sat in silence. "We will sit here" Hyacinth said, "We will sit here as long as we have to and wait for Wisteria."

Her tactic was to wear Violah out. She figured that if enough time passed Violah might break the silence and confess. This was her hope.

❄ Violah Plotting ❄

❀ Hyacinth consoles Azaelah ❀

But as days passed, it seemed clear to her that Violah was not about to budge. She needed to concentrate on the turning of events. The sisters finally started going about their business in a very doleful manner. There were no obvious clues, and all Hyacinth could eat, sleep, and think was "Where's Wisteria?"

�֎ "Where's Wisteria?" ✵

Violah seemed to enjoy watching her sisters suffer. It wasn't until Hyacinth mentioned that without Wisteria, there was no way they would ever be able to get into their great grandmother's trunk, that Viola realized the potential problem. Wisteria was the only one with hands small enough to reach into the old key hole and unlock the trunk. It was full of many extravagant items, all of which made Violah salivate. Did this mean that she might have to reveal Wisteria's whereabouts? Or have her reappear as mysteriously as she had disappeared?

And then an alarming thought struck Violah. What if it was too late?!

To be continued....

"We'll sit here as long as we have to and wait for Wisteria." ❧

Afterword

Thank you for enjoying these tales. There are many more to come. I'm sure you'd like to know what did indeed happen to little Wisteria and I have just started to unravel that mystery which I would love to share with you ... but Violah just walked into the room and is inquiring what it is that I am scribbling away about.

One minute...

Well now she has plopped herself in the corner and refuses to move because Hyacinth and Azaeleah are talking incessantly about poor Wisteria. It seems to have left Violah in a state of nausea. That being said, I think you and I know full well that my speaking of the triplets is on hold for now. Fear not, Book II will have much to tell about the triplets as well as introducing you to more of the Sisters Kane...including Miss Magnolia Kane, the troubled ice skater.

Until then, I bid you the kindest regards.

Christy Kane

About the Author:
Christy Kane graduated from NYU with a degree in photography.
She has been creating dolls and documenting their happenings
for centuries. To learn more or inquire about purchasing a doll of
your very own visit www.christykane.com